TROUBLE

Helen Chapman

RISING STARS

NASEN House, 4/5 Amber Business Village, Amber Close,
Amington, Tamworth, Staffordshire, B77 4RP

Rising Stars UK Ltd.
7 Hatchers Mews, Bermondsey Street, London SE1 3GS
www.risingstars-uk.com

Published 2011

Cover design: Burville-Riley Partnership
Illustrations: Bill Greenhead for Illustration Ltd. / iStock
Text design and typesetting: Geoff Rayner
Publisher: Gill Budgell
Publishing manager: Sasha Morton
Editorial consultants: Lorraine Petersen and Dee Reid
Editorial: Jane Wood

British Library Cataloguing in Publication Data.
A CIP record for this book is available from the British Library.

ISBN: 978-1-84680-976-7

Printed in the UK by Ashford Colour Press Ltd, Gosport, Hampshire

CONTENTS

MEET THE GANG-STARS!

Jacky

Tom

Natalie

Zeke

4

Aaron

?

Callum

Becca

Claire

5

Name:
Callum

Special skill:
Pop singing

Good at:
Showing off

Not so good at:
Thinking about anyone but himself

Other info:
He's got the looks, the voice and the talent, and a massive ego. He's his own biggest fan, and he counts on his cousin Aaron to be his next biggest fan.

PROFILES

Name:
Natalie

Special skill:
Playing, singing,
dancing, acting, you
name it ...

Good at:
Everything!

Not so good at:
There's nothing she's not good at,
which is most annoying, especially for
her brother Tom.

Other info:
Teachers think she's pale and sickly, kids
think she's weird, her brother thinks
she's embarrassing — and she thinks
she's a vampire!

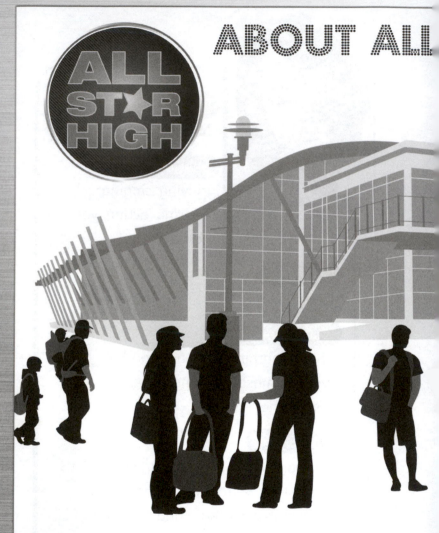

STAR HIGH

Do you want to be a star?
Then ALL STAR HIGH SCHOOL
is the place for YOU.
We will make you
a star.

Musicians,
dancers,
actors:
come see us now!

Don't miss out!

CHAPTER

There seemed to be something wrong
with Callum Murphy. He limped into
his drama class with one eye closed and
the other screwed up so he could hardly
see. He dumped his laptop and folder

on a table.

'Avast! Ahoy there!' he said in a loud voice.

Natalie Caplan looked up at him. 'Hello Callum,' she said. 'What's wrong with your leg?'

'Arrr,' said Callum. 'Arrr, matey.'

'What are you growling at me for? And don't call me matey,' said Natalie.

'I'm not growling,' said Callum. 'I'm talking like a pirate.' He opened his laptop. 'Look at this,' he said. 'Miss Spark has asked me to be in a contest to win a **lead role**.' He opened up his laptop and showed Natalie an email from Miss Spark, their drama teacher.

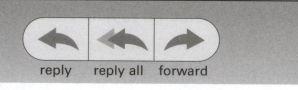

From: Spark@all-star-high.com

To: Murphy, Callum

Subject: BEST PIRATE CONTEST

ASH is putting on the musical *Pirates*. I want it to be special. Come to my next class and be the BEST PIRATE you can to WIN the LEAD ROLE!

'Open your eyes properly and look around you,' said Natalie. 'Everyone got that email. You're not the only one trying to be a pirate and win the contest.'

Callum opened his eyes properly and looked around him. Everyone had some sort of a pirate **prop**. Some had a **peg leg** and eye patch. Others had pirate scarves and earrings, or a fake hook for a hand. Some of them looked really good. They were making lots of 'arrr' noises.

Callum looked at Natalie again. Now that he had his eyes open properly, he could see that she was wearing weird clothes and earrings too. But then, Natalie always wore weird clothes and earrings. It was hard to tell if she was dressed as a weird pirate or just dressed as weird Natalie.

'I'm not into pirates,' said Natalie. 'That's why I'm not dressed up as a pirate. I don't mind what part I get in the show, as long as it's something interesting. But if you really want to win the contest and get the lead role, you'll need something special to make you stand out.'

'You're right,' said Callum. 'Everyone here is trying to be the best pirate. What can I do?'

Callum was a great singer and the best actor in the school. Natalie had never thought that he might need a bit of help to get a part.

'I'm sure I've got some props in my Bag of Tricks that could help you,' said Natalie. She always carried around a big bag full of weird props. The Gang-Stars called it Nat's Bag of Tricks.

Callum wasn't sure about letting Natalie help him. She had some weird ideas sometimes. What sort of props would she have? Maybe she wanted him to be a vampire pirate! Maybe she had a fake bat or some fake blood. He thought about a great pirate film that he had seen.* The actor played the role so well that his costume and props didn't matter. Callum made up his mind. He didn't need props either. He would get the lead role just by being the best actor, and everyone would remember him as the best pirate ever to be in a musical at All Star High.

'No thanks, Natalie,' he said. 'I don't want to use any of your props. I'll just use my acting to get the part.'

During the class the students all tried to be the best pirate they could. Miss Spark watched them act and sing. Callum was by far the best, and nobody was surprised when she gave him the

*The Pirates of the Caribbean films starring Johnny Depp as Captain Jack Sparrow.

lead role.

'You see,' said Callum, 'who needs props?'

For the rest of the class, Callum practised his acting and pirate lines.

'Yo-ho-ho, me hearties!'

'Arr, you scurvy dog!'

'Shiver me timbers!'

Natalie was going to play a pirate who creeps on to the ship and kidnaps a baby. For the rest of the lesson, she practised creeping around making no noise, and learning her kidnapping lines.

'Ssh! Be quiet!'

It didn't take her long to learn them!

But playing the part of the kidnapper was not very interesting and Natalie wanted to make it better. She didn't want more lines but she did want the audience to notice her. 'I've got to make this character special,' she thought. 'But how?'

CHAPTER

The rehearsals for *Pirates* took place over the next few weeks. The show was okay, but it wasn't anything special. Miss Spark watched the **dress rehearsal** on the day of the show and felt worried.

In a few hours the hall would be full of people and she still wasn't sure what to do to fix the play. 'I want it to sparkle,' she said.

Callum was on stage and he was worried too. Where was Natalie? He needed to rehearse a **scene** with her.

Suddenly there was a terrible screeching noise. Everyone went quiet and looked round in shock. Callum wasn't too surprised when he saw that Natalie and the noise arrived together. She was carrying something big, covered with a towel. Callum couldn't wait to see what was under the towel. Knowing Natalie, it could be anything.

'What is it?' he asked.

Natalie pulled the towel away like a magician doing a trick.

'Ta-da!' said Natalie. 'Meet Fred, the talking parrot. He's my Gran's pet but she's lending him to me for *Pirates*. My character needs something special so Fred will be with me.'

'Wow!' said Miss Spark. 'I think Fred might be the extra sparkle we need for this show.'

Natalie took Fred out of his cage. Fred jumped on to her shoulder and flapped his wings as Natalie walked up to Callum. Dust and tiny feathers went up into the air. Callum stepped back.

'You're not scared of a bird, are you?' asked Natalie.

'No, but I'm a bit ahh … ahh … **allergic** to … ATCHOO … feathers,' said Callum. His eyes began to water.

'Ahh … ahh … ATCHOO,' said Fred. Everyone laughed.

'Sshh! Be quiet!' said Natalie.

'Sshh! Be quiet!' said Fred. Everyone laughed again.

'There, he's learned our lines already,' said Natalie. 'I think I'd better keep Fred away from you, Callum. His feathers are making you sneeze really badly.'

Callum nodded to say yes, but he

kept sneezing. In between the sneezing he saw how everyone was fussing over Fred. Callum knew that Fred would get all the attention. The audience would love the parrot and just watch to see what it would do next. Callum felt annoyed. He wanted his acting to be the **highlight** of the musical, not a bird.

25

CHAPTER

The music began for the very last rehearsal and Callum forgot all about his feather allergy. He sang his first song while Fred sat still on Natalie's shoulder. Fred seemed to be watching

Callum and listening to him politely.

Everything was fine until Callum stopped singing. Fred always got a treat after sitting still on someone's shoulder. Where was his piece of fruit? Fred took off to find his treat. He **dive-bombed** into the cardboard pirate ship set and left a hole. Then he started chewing on the fake cannon balls.

'That parrot is wrecking the set!' said Miss Spark.

Natalie tried to pick up Fred but he just screeched, 'Shh! Be quiet!' Everyone laughed except Callum. He was really annoyed to see how much attention the parrot was getting, so he said, 'Come on, everyone, let's do that last bit again.' Then he started singing at the top of his voice to try and drown out the noise of the parrot.

Natalie put the parrot back in the cage while Callum kept singing. Fred stopped screeching and started to copy Callum singing. Now everyone laughed even more.

'What can we do?' asked Callum. 'The parrot will wreck the musical if he just keeps copying me like that.'

Miss Spark had an idea. 'I know what we can do,' she said. 'We'll only bring Fred on stage tonight for the last scene, when you aren't singing. He can stay in his cage in the **dressing room** for the rest of the time. Let's try it now.'

Callum thought this was a good idea.

Natalie thought it was a good idea.

Everybody at the final dress rehearsal thought it was a good idea.

But Fred didn't think it was a good idea at all.

The dressing room was cold and there was nobody there to talk to. But there were things to play with. Fred climbed down from his perch and pushed open the cage door. He flew out and started pecking the props and ripping the pirate flags to bits. When he heard voices, he flew back into the cage and pulled the door shut with his beak.

A boy with spiky red hair **swash-buckled** on to the stage.

'There's a big mess in the dressing room,' he said. 'Come and see.'

'Who was that?' Callum asked Natalie, as they went to see the dressing room.

'I don't know,' said Natalie. 'But he's right about the dressing room. Look at this.'

The dressing room was in an awful mess. Who could have done it?

'This is not good,' said Miss Sharp. 'Natalie, we can't have your parrot making this sort of trouble.'

'Don't blame Fred. It can't have been him,' said Natalie. 'His cage door is shut.'

Miss Spark looked at Fred. There was something that looked like a bit of a flag on his claws. But Natalie was right, his cage door was shut tight, so he couldn't have made the mess.

'Okay,' she said. 'I hope you're right. Come on, everyone. We need to finish the rehearsal quickly so you have time for a break before the show starts.'

They finished the rehearsal. The show was okay, but it still wasn't anything special. 'Everyone, you've got forty minutes to have a break and get something to eat before the show starts,' said Miss Spark. 'Leave your costumes tidy so you can find everything you need when you come back. Natalie, make sure that Fred's cage door is shut tight before you go.'

Natalie did as she was told and then went for her break.

Forty minutes later everyone came back to the dressing-room. The room was an even bigger mess than before. The costumes, wigs and make-up were no longer in neat piles. Now they were all over the place, and some of them were ripped.

This time Natalie knew that Fred was

to blame. There were feathers all over the room and Fred was out of his cage, sitting on a shelf with glitter all over his wings.

'This is terrible,' said Miss Spark. 'Hurry up, everyone. We haven't got time to sort out all the costumes. Just grab what you can.'

There were lots of scarves and wigs flying about the room. Fred was scared. He thought people were throwing things at him and so he flew up to a high shelf and wouldn't come down.

'Leave him,' said Miss Spark. 'The audience is waiting. You all need to get on stage.'

Most of the cast walked out on to stage wearing odd bits of costumes. There were girls with beards and boys with wigs. It looked like they had been playing in a dressing-up box.

The audience wasn't sure what was happening. They had never seen pirates quite like this before so they just clapped politely.

'Let's face it, Callum,' said Natalie. 'This show is in trouble before it's even started.'

Callum had to agree. But it was too late now.

'The show must go on,' he said.

CHAPTER

Callum started to say his lines. Suddenly, with a loud screech, Fred flew on to the stage. The audience clapped.

'Oh no! This can't be happening,' Callum thought.

It was time for Natalie to come
on stage and try to kidnap the baby.
Natalie looked at Fred as he swooped
across the stage. She had to say
something. Anything. She decided to
make up her own lines.

'Oh look,' she said, 'It's Fred, my
long-lost parrot. When I was a pirate
captain he flew away during a battle.'
Natalie realised that she didn't sound
like a pirate so she added, 'Arrr.'

Fred repeated: 'Arrr. 'Arrr.'

Everyone in the audience said, 'Arrr'
too, and there was lots of laughing.

Natalie ended her scene by trying to
pick Fred up. Fred screeched and flew off

above the audience. He flew higher and higher until he reached the ceiling. Two hundred black and white balloons were tied up and held by a net. They were there for the end of term party but Fred didn't know that. He grabbed on to the net with his claws.

On stage a battle started between the pirate ships. Callum called out: 'Load the cannonballs!'

At the same time Fred pecked at the net with his sharp beak. The net started to come loose.

'And fire!' shouted Callum.

Fred pecked the net again. The net gave way and the balloons started to float out. Fred pecked at the balloons. Pop! Pop! Pop! The noise startled Fred. He flapped his wings and started to peck wildly. POP! POP! POP! More balloons floated down on to the audience.

'Cannonballs!' they cried. The audience loved being part of the play. They grabbed the balloons, tossed them around and popped them loudly while the battle on stage carried on. Fred flew around, pecking more balloons and copying the noise of them popping. When all the balloons were gone, Fred swooped down and landed on Natalie's shoulder and the audience cheered.

Somehow, the show had gone from being nothing special to being a huge hit!

At the end of the show, Callum looked at Natalie. 'So, do you think you're going to get in trouble for all this?'

'No way,' said Natalie. 'Look at Miss Spark. Everyone is telling her how great *Pirates* was.'

Natalie was pleased with herself. She had made the musical more interesting, just like she wanted. Callum was pleased with himself, too. He had acted really well and kept the musical on track.

The audience was leaving, but one man stayed in his seat.

'Look! That's Oscar Lee,' said Callum. 'He's a **talent scout** and he's famous for finding new stars.'

'And he's coming over to me,' said Natalie.

'No, he's not,' said Callum. 'He's coming over to me.'

Oscar Lee walked up to Callum and Natalie.

'I know a great new talent when I see it,' he said. He held out his hand. They thought Oscar wanted to shake their hands but he didn't.

Fred jumped on to the talent scout's

hand. Oscar Lee held Fred right up to
his face.

'You're a very special bird,' he said. 'I
want to make you a star.'

GLOSSARY

allergic – being sensitive to something that can make you sneeze, get a rash or even make you very ill

dive-bomb – fly down fast to hit something, like a warplane

dress rehearsal –practising a show in full costume to check that everything works

dressing room – the room where actors get ready for a show

highlight – the best part of something

lead role – the part of the most important character in a show

limp – walk with difficulty because of a painful leg

peg leg – a wooden leg

props – short for 'properties'; objects used in a show

scene – a section of a play set in one particular place

scurvy – an illness that sailors used to get if they didn't have enough vitamins

swash-buckled – fast sword-fighting in a film or a show

talent scout – someone who looks for talented people to make them into stars

QUIZ

1 Who sent Callum the email about the contest?

2 What was the name of the musical they were going to put on?

3 What did Natalie's character have to do in the show?

4 What lines did Natalie have to learn?

5 What was the name of the parrot?

6 Who did the parrot belong to?

7 Why did Callum start to sneeze?

8 Who made the mess in the dressing-room?

9 Who was Oscar Lee?

10 Who did Oscar Lee want to make into a star?

ANSWERS

1   Miss Spark

2   *Pirates*

3   Kidnap a baby.

4   'Ssh! Be quiet!'

5   Fred

6   Natalie's Gran

7   Because he's allergic to feathers.

8   Fred the parrot.

9   A famous talent scout.

10 Fred the parrot.

ABOUT THE AUTHOR

Helen Chapman is an Australian author of eighty books who has been published in the United Kingdom, the U.S.A, New Zealand and Australia. She has travelled extensively and lived in America and England and is currently living in Australia.

For further information on Helen and her books visit: www.helenchapman.com

Helen has a special friend Rose Inserra who knows what her contribution has been to the ASH series and who can never be sufficiently thanked for it.

The All Star High books are available from most booksellers. For more information or to order, please call Rising Stars on 0800 091 1602 or visit www.risingstars-uk.com

RISING ★ STARS